NATHAN OF YESTERYEAR AND MICHAEL OF TODAY

BRIAN J. HEINZ

illustrated by JOANNE FRIAR

M Millbrook Press / Minneapolis

For Lennon Patrick,
as you create your own personal history
—B.H.

To my mother and father,
whose shared sense of history inspires me.
—J.F.

Millbrook Press, Inc.
A division of Lerner Publishing Group
241 First Avenue North
Minneapolis, MN 55401 U.S.A.

Website address: www.lernerbooks.com

Library of Congress Cataloging-in-Publication Data

Heinz, Brian J., 1946-
   Nathan of yesteryear and Michael of today / by Brian J. Heinz ; illustrated by Joanne Friar.
      p. cm.
   ISBN-13: 978–0–7613–2893–3 (lib. bdg. : alk. paper)
   ISBN-10: 0–7613–2893–9 (lib. bdg. : alk. paper)
1. United States—Social life and customs—Juvenile literature. 2. Social change—United States–Juvenile literature. 3. Technology—Social aspects—United States—Juvenile literature. 4. Technological innovations—United States—Juvenile literature. I. Friar, Joanne H. II. Title.
   E161.H45 2007
   303.4'00973—dc22   2005011054

Manufactured in the United States of America
1 2 3 4 5 6 – JR – 12 11 10 09 08 07

What do you know about the lives of your great-great-grandparents? Do you know their names? Do you know how they studied at school? Or what they did for fun?

Meet Nathan, who lived in this house 120 years ago. And meet Michael, Nathan's great-great-grandson, who lives in the same house, on the same street, today.

Time has passed, and change has followed. The world of Nathan and the world of Michael are quite different.

3

On an April day in yesteryear, Nathan casts his line and dangles his feet into the clear water of the millpond. There will be fresh trout for dinner. The miller waves to Nathan and raises a wooden gate, allowing the river to spill over the wheel of his gristmill. The playful splash of falling water is the natural power, the free energy, that drives the machinery. Inside the mill, shafts as thick as tree trunks begin to turn. Stout wooden teeth on huge wheels bite into each other, and the millstones roll against the grain, grinding out the wheat flour for today's bread.

Today Michael walks along the same river. Now it is lined with power plants and factories that hum twenty-four hours a day. Their stacks pierce the sky, pumping out the smoke and soot of burning coal and oil that provide the energy to run the machinery.

A great dam has replaced the old mill. Water roars as it surges past turbines to create electricity. The energy is delivered overland to faraway towns by cables strung on steel towers.

NO FISHING NO SWIMMING

In yesteryear, a barn raising for a new neighbor is under way. The entire village turns out to help. Nathan and his father yoke the oxen to a flat sled and drag stones from the field for the foundation. Whack! Thump! Axe and hammer ring against wood. Trees are felled one at a time. Logs are trimmed and pegs are driven to build a strong framework.

Wagons haul pine slabs from the mill. Bucksaws snarl to cut the planks into floorboards. Walls are raised by poles and pulleys and ropes, by muscle and sweat.

Nathan's mother sets plates of food on a makeshift table to satisfy growing appetites. A hundred hands are at work. They push, pull, dig, and scrape. They sweep, cut, cook, and chop. A fiddler's lively reel lightens spirits to lighten the work. At day's end, there are hugs and handshakes— and grateful tears for a job well done.

Michael stares at the steel skeleton that has
risen from a mammoth hole dug in the earth.
Workers swarm the girders like ants. Winches
whine as cranes hoist tons of brick, lumber, and
glass to dizzying heights. Trucks pour an ocean
of concrete. Twenty-four hours a day, the city
grows around him and above him. A forest of
trees has become a forest of skyscrapers.
Nathan's village has become Michael's city.

On a spring evening in yesteryear, young Nathan snuggles beneath a feather quilt and reads a favorite book of poetry. The glow from the fireplace and a flicker of a candle in a brass holder are all that light his page. It is hard on the eyes, and reading is slow. Through his open window, a soft breeze carries in the scent of lilacs. A lantern swings to the clip-clop rhythm of a horse-drawn carriage, splashing light on the country road that winds past the house.

Today, Michael lies in his bed and turns the pages of his favorite sci-fi novel. Reading is easy, because light is available at the flick of a switch.

Beyond his window, countless lights define the buildings and streets of a big city. The headlights of automobiles pierce the darkness like sabers, while shop signs and storefronts decorate the city in an electric dazzle of color.

Nathan enters the village square. The town crier announces the arrival of news. A rider swings down from his lathered horse. A mail pouch contains a few hand-scrawled letters that have taken weeks to reach their destination. Then the courier tacks a broadsheet to a wooden frame. There is excitement as Nathan reads aloud to the gathering crowd, for there are some who are unschooled and illiterate. The news is passed by mouth, from person to person to person. Nathan's town is too small for a telegraph office. There are no poles strung with wire to carry the strange clicks of Morse code, and there is yet no telephone. But these printed words speak of a new invention called radio that may send talking messages across the sea invisibly and in just moments.

"Impossible," shouts one man. "I don't believe it."

But Nathan wonders, Can it be true?

On a park bench, Michael slips his laptop from his backpack and flips up the screen. He pulls a PDA from his pocket to check his homework assignments.

People stroll by with elbows cocked and heads down, pressing tiny cell phones to their ears or smiling at images on camera phones.

The steel grids of satellite towers soar above the trees, adding a new feature to the horizon as they bounce signals into space.

Beep! Beep! Michael grabs his pager from a belt clip. It's a text message. He taps out a response and, with the stroke of a fingertip, sends it into cyberspace.

Nathan walks his dog by the waterfront of yesteryear. There is the smell of tar on the rigging of schooners that rock gently with furled sails. Laborers nod their greetings and tread the gangplanks, bent under crates of wine and bales of cotton from distant lands. Teamsters guide draft horses from heavily laden wagons, their iron-strapped wheels clattering over the cobblestones. Nathan leaps aside as a gentleman pedals past on his high-wheeled velocipede.

A coach rolls up to deposit passengers and luggage headed to Europe on a sleek clipper ship. An acre of canvas will capture the wind to drive the vessel over the ocean. Other passengers will await the docking of the faster but more costly steam packet ship that will get them across the ocean in less than two weeks. Incredible! A steam locomotive hoots from the hill behind town, chugging along at the breakneck speed of 20 miles (32 kilometers) per hour. Nathan heads home, traveling as he does best. Walking.

CORIOLANUS

How the harbor has changed for Michael! Cruise ships, like floating cities, carry thousands of travelers with all the comforts of home. The tracks now carry high-speed trains that whip over the countryside at 200 miles (320 kilometers) per hour. Overhead, a jumbo jet heads across the ocean, destined to reach Europe in a matter of hours. Michael dodges the motorcycles weaving through traffic.

Today's teamsters haul goods in ten-ton trucks, while aerodynamic automobiles with high-tech instruments zip along elevated superhighways.

Nathan awoke early for his four-mile (6.5 kilometer) walk, through field and forest, from home to school. He clomps up the steps of the yesteryear schoolhouse. "Good morning, Miss Pratt," he shouts. His teacher nods and continues to yank the bell rope. The clang from the belfry calls her students to class.

The school is but a single room with benches and desks bolted to the floor. Miss Pratt arrived at dawn to start a coal fire in the potbellied stove, the only source of heat.

Jackets hang from pegs, lunch bags sit on a shelf. Children are arranged in rows according to their age and grade. Nathan slides into the fifth row. He scratches out arithmetic in chalk on a slate tablet and holds it up for the teacher's approval. Later, Nathan practices his penmanship. Dipping a quill into the inkwell in his desk, he shapes his letters in delicate lines of sepia. A sprinkling of fine sand over the coarse paper blots the excess ink. Miss Pratt nods her approval.

Students spill from a caravan of yellow buses at the curb beside a sprawling brick school. Michael is among them. He bounds up the steps, runs to his hall locker, and tosses in his hat. Student lunch menus are posted on each door. Hmm-m-m, spaghetti with garlic bread in the cafeteria today.

A buzzer beckons students into their classrooms. As Michael takes his seat, a wall speaker barks the morning announcements. Then the teacher flips a switch. An overhead projector lights the screen with today's lesson. Students start their desktop computers and go to work. Fingers tap on plastic keyboards, and digital images march across the screen. Michael finishes and hits a command key. Like magic, across the room, his work peels out from a laser printer and falls into a waiting tray near the teacher's desk.

On a Saturday in November, neighbors arrive for a yesteryear evening of fun. The children sit scattered over the braided rug pulling gobs of vanilla taffy. Nathan shakes popcorn in a long-handled pan over the fire. Parents and grandparents clutch mugs of hot cocoa while they enjoy Mother's piano playing.

Time is passed in card games, checkers, or chess. As the fire dims and the autumn wind moans, Nathan's grandfather settles into his oak rocker, a signal for the eager youngsters to gather 'round to hear a well-told ghost story.

Today Michael entertains himself in a sea of electronic gadgetry. What will it be today? The plasma screen HDTV, a CD, the DVD, or maybe he'll download some new music into his iPod? And there's a new thriller at the multiplex cinema. Of course, he's itching to play that hot, interactive computer game he recently downloaded onto his PC. A palm-held video game chatters in bleeps and blips as Michael concentrates on saving Earth from an alien invasion.

Nathan and his family are dressed and gathered at the table for dinner. It is a social event, a time for fathers, mothers, sons, and daughters to catch up on one another's lives in conversation. What happened in school today? At work? At home? There is laughter and the tousling of hair. There are warm hearts and steaming food. Mother spent hours preparing the meal, but it is a labor of love that is evident in every bowl and every bite. Spiced apples bubble beneath a golden crust. A sizzling roast is drawn from the oven, basted in sweet juice, and neatly sliced. Sesame rolls line the bread tray. Carrots and potatoes, pulled from the garden this morning, are heaped on a platter and slathered in butter. It is a feast for the eye and the nose, as well as the belly. It is Nathan's turn to say grace, to give thanks. And no one is in a hurry.

Today it is take-out time. Michael must choose. Chinese egg rolls and wonton soup? Japanese sushi? Italian pasta or pizza? Maybe a Mexican five-alarm chili and tacos smothered in jack cheese? Perhaps just a burger and fries. Phone your orders day or night, and fast-food jockeys scurry to your door. Family dinners are a shared sampling of international goodies. Tonight there are things to do and places to go. Aerobics class at the gym for Mom and a community meeting for Dad. Karate and soccer practice for Michael and his sister. The clock is ticking. Michael and his family chow down on fried chicken and lick their fingers clean.

Times have changed.

Nathan and Michael have lives quite different from each other.
But they both have their hobbies, their work, their skills, and their
dreams. They have their pets and their friends and their families.

Some things never change.